A TRACE OF DEATH

BY

MARTIN GROVES

A TRACE OF DEATH

BY

MARTIN GROVES

Book Cover by Tony Merkel

Dedicated to those whom have lost their lives or are missing due to encounters with these beasts in our National Parks and Recreation Areas.

INTRODUCTION

In the year of 1993 my hunting partner Harry and myself entered into the Land Between the Lakes Recreation area. We traveled there for the purpose of Spring Turkey hunting and backwoods camping. It was a beautiful spring in the L.B.L. with flowers and greenery and wildlife everywhere. The birds were singing and the creeks were alive with aquatic life. We found a great campsite in the extreme backwoods of the Devil's Backbone. We did not realize what he had set in motion by the choice of our campsite. Harry and I were avid back country campers and hunters. Both of us having visited the L.B.L. and other backwoods of Kentucky and Tennessee. We had been raised hunting and fishing since we were both small boys. In 1993 neither of us had ever heard of local legends nor considered ourselves BIGFOOT believers. From what we both knew at that time our mentality was that if there were indeed BIGFOOT they lived in the California Redwoods or Washington state. There was nothing like that in Kentucky or Tennessee and if there were we absolutely was not afraid of it. However, before our hunting trip was finished our outlook upon the phenomenon of BIGFOOT or the local legend of DOGMAN would be changed forever. The hunting trip would turn into a horrifying event that would leave Harry and myself scared mentally for the rest of our life, and leave my friend Harry physically impaired for life ending his career in law enforcement. It would cause me to spend the next thirty years of my life in pursuit of truth investigating this phenomenon. I would interview over two hundred witnesses and investigate hundreds of sites searching for evidence such as tracks, hair and DNA samples. I would lead many expeditions into Land Between the Lakes and even National Parks where witnesses and events that would be reported to me. I did this in total secrecy never seeking any recognition or notoriety by the public. The following is an account of some of the witnesses and their direct contact with the phenomenon of BIGFOOT and DOGMAN. You will also learn of what took place in the Devil's Backbone that changed my entire belief of what these beasts are and possibly where they live. Join me on this epic adventure, listen to what some of the witnesses have to say.

Aerial View of Land Between the Lakes

A Trace of Death

Chapter 1

It is said that the peninsula known as the Land Between the Rivers is as old as time itself. Its most beautiful rolling hills, the green pastures and woods have been home to the American Indian tribes and the first pioneers that settled the area. Its beauty and charm warm the hearts and souls of many. The isles and bays are for sportsmen and hunters. It speaks to the souls of us all giving each person a different call, for some it's the CALL OF THE WILD for others its thrill of camping outdoors or a holiday to make memories. For some it's the allure of nature, the beautiful flowers and wildlife that inhabits the 171,000 plus acres of nature's delight. However, this land also holds another side that most people will never know. The story is told that of a dark and sinister nature that lurks in the shadows of the forest, that stalks the creeks and rivers. It is said that tales of the beast dates back to the days of the Cherokee and Shawnee. That a man beast described as half man half wolf hunts the lands known as the DARK AND BLOODY GROUND. The tribes tell of a Shawnee medicine man or Shaman that could shapeshift into a wolf beast that fed upon the animals or members of the tribe. That the tribal hunters gathered to track and kill this beast that fed upon the children. They captured the Shaman while in his wolf beast state as he was devouring one of their own. It is said they killed the beast and as it lay on the ground dying the Shaman changed from beast to man in front of them, cursing them and the land and vowing he would return and seek vengeance upon them and others and to forever haunt the DARK AND BLOODY GROUNDS.

The French fur trappers working for the Transylvania Fur Company reported of dark shadowy figures that lurked the forest and hunted them. They would find members of their hunting party slain in the woods with their throats torn out and their organs eaten. They spoke of strange mysterious lights that would follow and stalk the hunters in the woods and fields. As they camped by their fires they would hear the dark moan-full howls of a beast they had never heard before. The trappers would find deer and buffalo with their throats ripped open and only the soft organs eaten from the animals. Even their own horses fell prey to these wolf beasts. Sometimes they would find members of their own party slain, slaughtered in the same manner. Sometimes the trappers and hunters would simply disappear without a trace of them ever found.

There have been consistent tales of these wolf beast sightings going back over three hundred years. With these stories or tales being passed from mouth to-ear, passed down from generation to generation these tales of a massive wolf beast that stands over six to seven feet tall that walks on two legs. The beast is covered in thick matted fur and smells like death itself. Its eyes as red as the coals of hell itself and its mouth displaying huge razor sharp teeth for ripping and tearing its victims.

Others claim the beast comes from a family that traveled from EUROPE and settled within the Land Between the Rivers. That this family were in fact werewolves and that they hunted the area in pursuit of flesh. That members of this family, its descendants still lurk in the the park and surrounding areas in search of campers, hunters and fishermen or anyone when the opportunity arises for them to feed upon their flesh.

No matter what the beast is, the stories still persists of farmers that have lost their livestock. Wherever the gathering they speak of having their chickens, cows, pigs even their horses and mules killed. They sometimes find their animals killed, slain in the most hideous ways. That of having their heads ripped off, their necks torn or sliced open. In many of these cases it appears that the beast or beasts killed or murdered the animal for sheer sport or delight based on the fact the animals would not be eaten. The farmers state as if their animals were killed merely for the act itself.

Then we have the stories from a variety of sources that the beast also hunts humans. There are modern stories of campers, fisherman hikers and hunters that have been found predated upon. And we have sightings reported by upstanding members of the surrounding communities that continue to this very day that report seeing the wolf man like beast stalking the shadows of the forest, lakes and campgrounds. It is true that long before modern day roads existed, long before the road was named the TRACE that connects DOVER, TENN and GRAND RIVERS, KENTUCKY we can say then and now it is a TRACE OF DEATH.

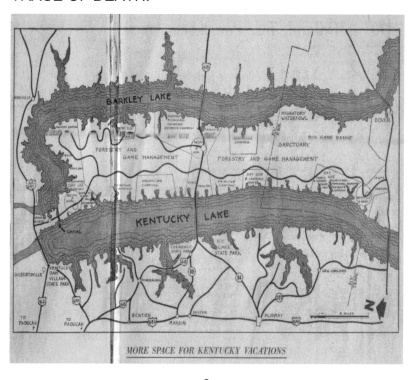

MORE SPACE FOR KENTUCKY VACATIONS

The Shaman Changes

Chapter 2

If you take a map and compare the encounters and events that has taken place from the area around Land Between the Lakes, you can form a triangle of events. Almost like the one of the ALASKA triangle of where you have terrible events of missing persons, hunters attacked or killed. Reports of crashed airplanes with missing pilots that reported they crashed and needed help but they were never found. Since my own personal encounter in the year of 1993 I have researched or investigated every report I could find or has been given to me by witnesses. In many cases the witnesses themselves were what we refer to as first - hand accounts or witness. Having encountered some form of beast or had a sighting within the park itself or on the outskirts of it. I have talked with hundreds of witnesses that simply want to report what had happened to them or to their family. One common factor among them all was that in most cases they feared reprisal or ridicule by their peers or community. Many of these good folks, what I call upstanding citizens stated to me the same thing. They knew full well that if they talked or reported their encounter or events they would be ostracized by their community. It is as simple as this, the park itself generates over five million dollars in revenue with millions of dollars in business, hotels and restaurants. It is also reported that over eight million dollars in government grants are given. One witness told me that he had reported a strange event and had a local mayor came to his business and ask him to recant his story that it was bad for local folks trying to make a living off of the tourist trade. Now rest assured the last thing I would ever want is to cause any distain among the tourist trade or cause problems for any reason. With that said it is my belief that no price can be put on a human life. No matter what the stories are the facts are plain and simple something is taking place within this triangle. Let me share with you some of the statements of various witnesses.

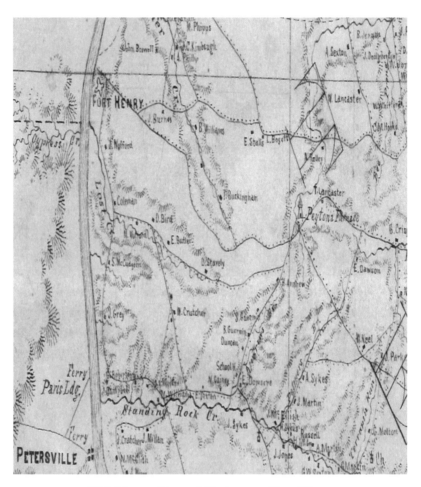

Old Map of Land Between the Rivers

The Witnesses

Chapter 3

All of my adult life I have trained to be a Police Officer an Investigator of the truth. I have been trained to investigate everything you can imagine. From a traffic wrecks, minor or major to fatalities. I have been trained and certified to investigate any crime that could occur from minor or major crimes, personal crimes, homicides or suicides. I never thought that one day I would use that same ability to investigate some type of paranormal or cryptid events. My life changed after my encounter in L.B.L after 1993 I began to look into this strange phenomenon. I spent all of my off-duty time within this area talking with, speaking to locals about strange sightings, attacks or missing persons and even crimes ranging from murder or suicides. Anything concerning the citizens. I would gather around anywhere the locals went, anywhere hunters and fisherman would sit down and share stories and drink coffee or grab a snack. It was very easy for me to fit in among everyone. After all I was in many ways one of them. I had been raised hunting and fishing in this area. We would always pay our respects on Memorial Day, or celebrate the 4th of July and holidays. Some folks knew my family and told me stories of old when there was no TVA. Some folks knew I was a law enforcement officer from another county, those whom did not if they asked me, I would tell them where I worked. The majority of folks did not care as I was one of them. Over a course of 30 years I sat and listened to their stories, even visited in their homes or sit outside and sip tea or coffee as they re-told their stories to me. Most folks wanted to remain anonymous in fear of reprisal. I kept my promise to them and never spoke of their names or where they lived. They spoke of first-hand accounts or stories of their family and what had happened to them within the park. Let me share some of these with you.

WITNESS TOM

Chapter 4

I will never forget one of the first stories I heard in 1993 from a fisherman from Dover, Tn. I met him at store that was on the TRACE RD. I got to know Tom very well over the years and discovered he was a fine upstanding member of his community and folks knew him to be a truthful man.

Tom reported to me that in April of 1989 he and his cousin Jake had been fishing on the Kentucky Lake side of L.B.L. that they had a good day fishing catching some crappie and bluegills. They had fished all day long and had grown tired, it was getting late and the sun was about to set. Tom stated he had parked his truck and boat trailer in an area known as ST. MARY'S. It was a small boat ramp in the back woods area. Tom stated it was just enough light to get to the ramp and pull up onto the shore, Tom jumped out of the boat and went walking up the hill to retrieve his Ford pick-up truck and back down to get the boat. Tom stated that he had a very eerie feeling as he was walking, like he was being watched so it made him a little jittery. He stated this was a very remote area and very few people use this ramp. Tom stated as he was backing down to the ramp he heard Jake screaming at him, look out Tom. He put the truck in park and stepped out of the truck, as he was stepping out of the truck he immediately heard gunshots. What he saw next was horrifying to him. Jake was standing up in the boat and had emptied his 22-caliber pistol at a wolf like, bi pedal beast that stood approximate seven feet tall. Tom said the beast was not affected and that it ran toward him and up the side of the embankment. Further that another beast was standing above him by the entrance to the graveyard of St. Mary's cemetery. Tom stated he kept his eyes on the beast for what seemed like an eternity, then the beast simply ran off on two legs. Jake began screaming for him to come get him. Tom opened up his truck door and pulled out his shotgun and watched the area for a few moments. Jake was insisting that he back down to get the boat and "Let's get out of here". He stated they retrieved the boat and fled the area. The following day he reported the incident to the local fish and wildlife officer whom insisted that they had been a victim of a prank and that Jake must have not hit anyone. The officer stated he would check the local hospitals to see if anyone reported a gunshot wound and would get back with him. Tom stated he never heard anything else. As Tom related his story to me, he insisted that he was not the only one that had an encounter in this same area, that he has heard of others.

Photo by Dewey Edwards © 2023

St. Mary's Cemetery
Photo by Dewey Edwards © 2023

Boat Ramp @ St. Mary's
Photo by Dewey Edwards © 2023

St. Mary's Cemetery
Photo by Dewey Edwards © 2023

St. Mary's Cemetery
Photo by Dewey Edwards © 2023

The Beast of ST. MARY'S

Chapter 5

It goes without saying that after meeting Tom and hearing his story, I could not let it go. Tom had given me another name of a fellow fisherman and hunter that lived in the area. Tom said this man was a friend that went to the same church and that he had seen the beasts at the SAINT MARY'S cemetery.

Tom arranged for me to meet with a man named James. I met with him at a location within L.B.L. at the old Confederate Fort Henry. I met with James in the month of October of 1994. James and I exchanged pleasantries and made the decision to travel to the location of St. Mary's cemetery. Upon location, James began to tell me the story of his encounter.

James stated that since he was a very young boy he had been a raccoon hunter. That in January of 1991 he had decided to park beside the gravel road next to SAINT MARY'S cemetery. James stated he had brought his six coon hounds and his trusty 22-caliber rifle. He was supposed to meet another hunter at this location just before dark. James had hunted with the same man for over 20 years that he and Phillip would often meet at this location. When Phillip did not show up James decided to release his dogs thinking that at any moment Phillip would arrive. Almost immediately James' lead dog King began to sound out indicating he was on a trail. Then King and all the others began barking and howling and James knew they had treed a raccoon.

James looked at his watch and made the decision that Phillip would see his truck and know to follow the barking in the woods and would join him. James grabbed his rifle and flashlight and entered the woods heading toward KING'S barking. James believed his hounds were approximately one half-mile or further from the truck. James started out at a fast pace to get to his dogs. Within a few moments he heard a noise that sent shivers up his spine. He heard his dogs fighting and whimpering and he could hear his hounds being attacked. Before he could get to the tree where they were located two of his dogs came running past him headed toward the truck. James continued to his dogs. He continued to hear one of his dogs squealing and whimpering as if in pain. James thought to himself it must be one mean bad raccoon to have sent two of his dogs running and the rest in painful moans. James stated he arrived at the tree and discovered two of his prized hounds lay dead on the ground lying in blood. He heard above him KING whimpering and immediately observed that he was impaled through his stomach on a tree branch. He then seen movement out of his right eye and looked over and to his shock and horror observed a large bi-pedal wolf creature standing approximate 6 foot to 7 feet in height holding one of his hounds in its right hand or claws, the hound was lifeless. James stated all he could do was stare at this creature or beast. The Beast was staring at him exposing its canine teeth. James stated he raised his Marlin 22 rifle and emptied it at the creature. He stated it simply ran off carrying away his hound. At the same time, he heard a noise behind him and realized it was his friend Phillip. Phillip was in total shock at what he was seeing and told James he had found the other two hounds underneath the truck and new something was wrong and he heard the shots and came running. James stated that Phillip had to climb up and remove KING from the branch in the tree. KING was in bad shape with his intestines exposed and in pain. Phillip took out his pistol and immediately dispatched the hound. James and Phillip could not believe what had just taken place. When James asked if Phillip had seen the Beast, Phillip replied he had seen something a large figure running away. It was like a large shadow on two legs. The two men stood there staring at the carnage and were both speechless. James was extremely upset having lost four of his best hounds. And KING, he was more than just a coon hound, he was like a family member.

James stated that after a few minutes they made the decision they should leave the area for their own safety. Phillip picked up KING and carried him back to the trucks. James stated that they laid KING in the bed of his truck on a blanket, placed the other two hounds in their box locking them in. James reloaded his rifle and Philip grabbed his rifle out of his own truck and they headed back to retrieve the other two hounds. James stated they were approximately a ten-minute walk through the woods to where the incident had taken place. That by the time they arrived back at this tree the two slain hounds were gone. This sent shivers into both the men because they knew the Beast had come back to take the hounds. As they were standing there a murderous scream almost like a wolf howl rattled the woods very close to them. Phillip fired one round from his rifle into the air and the woods went silent. The two men then walked in sheer terror back to their trucks and left.

James stated he reported this incident the next day to his local fish and wildlife officer. The officer stated to him he was sorry about his prized dogs. But it was obvious they had been attacked by a pack of coyotes, and that the one in the tree had attempted to escape by jumping into the tree and became impaled on a tree branch when it fell. James stated the officer basically would not hear or listen about what had taken place, writing it off as a coyote attack. James stated that KING was over 10 feet off the ground that there was no way his dog had climbed or jump up that high. James further told me that it was as if the hound was impaled on the branch for the sheer enjoyment by this murderous BEAST that had attacked his coon hounds. He further stated he had some more hunters that I could talk with that had or knew of the same kind of attacks within the park.

Over the years of knowing James he did in fact put me in touch with many hunter/witnesses in this area.

St. Mary's Cemetery
Photo by Dewey Edwards © 2023

The Coon Hunt
Photo by Dewey Edwards © 2023

The Death Tree
Photo by Dewey Edwards © 2023

The Impaling Tree
Photo by Dewey Edwards © 2023

St. Mary's Cemetery
Photo by Dewey Edwards © 2023

The Dogman's Retreat
Photo by Dewey Edwards © 2023

The Dogman Trail
Photo by Dewey Edwards © 2023

The Beast of Fort Henry

Chapter 6

During the month of October of 1994 I made a contact with a man by the name of Randy. He stated that he was a hiker and loved the history of the area. That he often traveled to Fort Henry and hiked the area. Randy stated that in the month of September of this year (1994) he had been hiking and searching the beach area around the old FORT. That it was late in the afternoon almost when the sun was setting, just before dusk. He had been staring down at the shoreline at the water's edge when he heard something in the woods in the area behind him. The woods were about 150 yards away from him but that he could see very large shadows between the trees. The shadows were using the trees as cover and he thought to himself that animals usually don't move in this manner. Randy kept walking but watched the woods line. It seemed as though the shadows moved only when he moved, stopped when he stopped walking. This kind of freaked him out a little. He kept walking but was attempting to keep sight of the figures in the woods and trying not to be obvious he was turning around to watch them. Randy stated that it was getting very close to dusk and knew he should attempt to get to his car parked at the trailhead. What happened next sent him into total shock. As he was leaving the shoreline the figures in the woods actually paralleled his movement. Then one of the figures stepped out of the wood line. It stood over six or seven feet in height, its fur was black and more like long matted hair. Randy stated it had a dog's head with a short snout. All of a sudden it raised its head and howled like a wolf, that made take off running. Randy ran all the way back to his car and just as he was about to get in, he looked up. He looked over to the other side of his Honda and saw two of the same type of Beasts standing approximate 50 yards away staring at him, as if they had been there waiting for him. Randy stated he jumped into his car and sped out of the area driving to the Park station located off the FORT HENRY road at the Highway 79 location to report the incident. Upon his arrival at the station the Ranger on duty told him he was mistaken about the animals he had seen. That they get reports all the time of coyotes chasing hikers in the woods, and that the coyotes often lurk around the gravel parking areas searching for food or garbage.

After meeting with Randy and considering that it had only been approximately one month ago. I immediately drove over to FORT HENRY. I parked in the very same parking lot and walked over to the shore of KENTUCKY LAKE. I began searching for tracks in the shoreline. It wasn't long before I found what I believed to be Randy's tracks. I followed the tracks to where I observed that he had stopped, changed direction turning back to return to his car. At first his tracks indicated he was walking, then running with a longer gate and on his toes / front of his foot. But what was even more interesting is finding huge bi-pedal wolf tracks three times the size of any coyotes, following him from the shore line into the woods and the hiking trail. After a few feet onto the trail itself I lost the wolf tracks but could easily follow through the woods the broken branches of said animal. The trail left by this animal went directly toward the gravel parking area for the trailhead of FORT HENRY. This was enough to lead me to believe the statement of this witness.

Fort Henry
Photo by Dewey Edwards © 2023

Fort Henry Trailhead
Photo by Dewey Edwards © 2023

Randy's Destination
Photo by Dewey Edwards © 2023

Fort Henry Parking Lot
Photo by Dewey Edwards © 2023

The Beast of the Devil's Backbone

Chapter 7

This next witness came to me through a Pastor of a local church off the Trace Road. The Pastor stated he had been given my name by some friends and thought that I might be able to help one of his members of the church. I agreed to meet with them and a date was set to meet at the church.

I met with them just before Christmas, December of 1994.

Christy stated she lived just outside of Dover, Tennessee That her family had lived in the state of Indiana. But that she moved to this area because of Land Between the Lakes and its beauty. Christy went on to tell me of her brother Derrick. That Derrick was 32 years old when he had died in L.B.L. in the year of 1987. Derrick would take his vacations and come visit with her and would often hike the trails along the TRACE. She said that her brother was in excellent physical condition and was an excellent hiker and sportsman. Derrick had served in the ARMY and had great skills in the woods. Christy went on to tell me that Derrick had left her house to go on a weekend hike along the Devil's Backbone and would return on Monday spending the weekend camping / hiking by himself. This was normal for him. Monday came and by nightfall Christy became worried about her brother and called the L.B.L. authorities. She said that a search was conducted and her brother's car was found parked at the trailhead. That they found his tent and belongings a few miles into the trail where he had slept. A search was conducted and her brother was not found, a subsequent search was conducted but he was never found. Many months passed and they had no word from the authorities. Then in the spring of 1988 word came to her that the remains of a body had been found but they were awaiting confirmation. Within a few weeks she was contacted and told that the remains were in fact her brother. That it appeared Derrick had died of a heart attack and animals had carried off and spread his bones in the immediate area. Christy and her family at first accepted this information. Until July of 1989 when she had been contacted by a so called concerned officer by telephone. He would not identify himself and told her that her brother had been killed by some type of animal. That he had been on the original search team and had found his tent ripped to shreds. That the tent showed evidence he was attacked in his sleep and a trail of blood leading into the deep woods. He stated they could not find his body anywhere. The caller stated he had resigned from his position and just wanted the family to know about her brother. Christy stated she attempted to get more information from him but he said that he was sorry and hung up. Christy stated the call came from a local pay phone.

I listened to Christy's story, taking all her information and assured her I would make every effort to obtain more information concerning Derrick. I did make all inquiries with local authorities and even newspaper accounts. I was told by authorities of the park that no records existed and if it was a natural death as a heart attack they would not keep anything concerning the incident. I continued to pursue all avenues of inquiries and informed Christy of any leads I had. A few years passed and I was informed she had died in a car collision in 1998. Christy died never finding out the truth about her brother. I pray she was reunited with him in heaven.

Derrick's Campsite @ Devil's Backbone
Photo by Dewey Edwards © 2023

Derrick's Demise
Photo by Dewey Edwards © 2023

Campfire

Derrick's Death Camp

Beasts of Buffalo Trace

Chapter 8

In March of 1995 I was visiting a local store when a local woman in Dover, Tennessee, overheard me speaking with a hunter concerning a sighting of a Beast on Highway 79. The lady identified herself as Sally and set down beside of me and the hunter. She stated that on weekends she travels from Dover, Tennessee to Cadiz, Kentucky to visit her family. Sally stated that in the month of May of 1993 she had got off of work late but decided to travel to Cadiz no matter of the time. She stated she turned on the TRACE road around midnight traveling north. That when she got close to the buffalo prairie she saw something that took her attention. Sally pulled onto the gravel parking area and shined her car lights toward the buffalo because she noticed the buffalo had formed a semi-circle around their calves. What she saw next totally shocked and terrorized her very soul. Sally described to me the following details.

I observed the herd of buffalo in a semi-circle around their calves, there were three bi-pedal wolf like Beasts standing in front of the buffalo. The beasts stood about six feet tall and their hands were in front of them like in an attack stance they were pacing back and forth facing the buffalo like they were attempting to find an opening to the smaller calves. Sally stated that due to the fence around the buffalo she felt safe and opened her car door and stood outside the vehicle. She just could not believe what she had seen. The Beasts were so occupied with the buffalo they seem to ignore her presence. The only thing she could think of doing was to blow her car horn at the Beasts and maybe run them off. I then hit the horn with one loud continuous blast. Then I hit the horn with a secession of blasts which seem to annoy the Beasts.

That's when the Beasts turned toward me, I started to get into my vehicle when I heard something from behind me a noise from the woods on the side of the road. I then observed a huge large Beast running on all fours headed in my direction. I jumped into my vehicle and sped out I could see the beast running behind me, I must have been doing over 55 mph and it seemed to be catching up with tremendous speed so I floored my accelerator and never looked back. I drove to my family's house in Cadiz and told them about the incident. My uncle contacted the authorities the following morning. He was told that it was only coyotes, that they had a lot of trouble with them attempting to take calves.

Bison Range
Photo by Dewey Edwards © 2023

Bison Range
Photo by Dewey Edwards © 2023

Bison Range Parking Lot
Photo by Dewey Edwards © 2023

Beasts of the Buffalo Pastures

Chapter 9

I first met Jerry within the park, in the 1980s. We had become friends and he gave me great locations to hunt deer. He had worked for years in the park as an agricultural worker. Jerry mowed fields and roadways and performed other tasks. He mowed fields and made hay for the animals within the park. In the summer of 1995 he had been mowing a field with his tractor to make hay rolls. He was in the area of the buffalo range. An area rich with grass and it made excellent hay. Jerry stated it was late afternoon and he was in a hurry as rains were coming later in the week. As he was making a turn beside the woods area he felt a thud and he knew his bush hog had run over something in the field. Jerry said it was common to hit a young fawn or other animals as he mows because they hide so well in the tall grass. He just kept mowing thinking when he came back around he would eventually see what he had struck. All of a sudden he caught something moving outside the cab of this tractor, he looked down and observed a large wolf-like beast running beside of him and that it was on two legs. Jerry stated it was attempting to open the door handle and that it was huge. He estimated the Beast as standing almost 7 to 8 feet in height. It had black matted fur and it obviously was a female because he could see breasts on its belly through his glass door. Jerry stated that he got scared and was in fear it would break the glass and get inside, he could see its teeth and that it was vicious. The only thing he could think of was to turn the wheel and attempt to hit the Beast with the tractor, he jerked the wheel to the left and the Beast slid down the side of the tractor and its legs hit the rear tires. Jerry said it rolled on the ground and got up. He gave the tractor full power and left the field. He believed that he had ran over the Beast's pups and it was chasing him down. He drove to the shop to report to his supervisor what had taken place. He was told to take the rest of the day off and not to speak of the incident. The following day when he returned to work. His supervisor told him he had ran over some coyote pups and their mother. The coyote was a very large one. Jerry stated he was told to move to another location and continue his mowing in other fields. Jerry was advised not to speak of the incident with anyone. Jerry retired from the park in 1996.

Field where Jerry was mowing
Photo by Dewey Edwards © 2023

Hay Rolls

Tractor similar to what Jerry was using

Park Ranger breaks his Silence.

Chapter 10

I met Officer Graves in 1989, he joined my local chapter of the Fraternal Order of Police. Graves lived within my area where I was the President of the organization. Graves became a loyal member and came to the monthly meetings when he could. Over the years we talked of many things, mostly about good hunting or fishing spots at the L.B.L. Officer Graves always set and talked with me after the meetings. One night in July of 1995, I could tell something was on his mind. Graves stated he was getting ready to retire. He told me that he was turning in his retirement papers and that this would be his last month. Graves waited until everyone left and asked if we could talk about something that was bothering him. The following was the substance of that conversation.

Graves stated for many years he had worked at the park. That he had to check many areas and do what he called security checks at certain stations where the public was not allowed to enter. That he also was responsible for checking electrical sub-stations. Graves stated he had seen many strange things in these areas. That the scientist had been tracking some kind of hybrid animals, to be exact some typo of large wolf. Graves stated that he would see K-9 type wire cages on the windows of large white cargo vans but was not permitted to get close to the vans if they passed into these security stations. He knew something was not right due to the secrecy. Graves stated that he knew that some hunters had been attacked and he believed it had something to do with these large wolves. He stated he was glad he was retiring and would have nothing more to do with it. I did attempt to gather further data from him, but I respected him when he stated he could not talk further about it. Mr. Graves did retire in 1995 and passed away in 1997.

Bridge to Cadiz KY

Dogman Hybrid

Dogman of LBL

TVA Ranger Badges

Witness Linda

Chapter 11

Linda contacted me via an e-mail I had posted for witnesses to contact me. Linda stated that she frequently places flowers on her family's graves in St Mary's cemetery. That in the month of May of 1995 she was visiting the cemetery. It was a beautiful afternoon in Land Between the Lakes and she was looking forward to seeing the trees and flowers that grow around the cemetery and decorate the graves with fresh flowers. Linda exited her car and had taken flowers out of the back seat and began to approach the graves when she noticed something moving in the back part of the cemetery. She could see two shadowy figures bent over one of the older graves. The two figures were digging at the graves and dirt was actually flying up into the air, Linda rubbed her eyes and positioned herself to block the sun and get a better look. She dropped her flowers in complete horror when one of the figures stood up standing over 7 feet tall covered in matted hair. The figure had a canine wolf like head and turned to look at her. Linda stated she began to walk backwards toward the car, keeping her eyes upon the creature. The other creature also stood up and turned her way and both began walking toward her. Linda ran for her car and made a hasty exit from the cemetery looking at her rearview mirror, she could see the two wolf creatures standing at the entrance of the cemetery. Linda recalled how large and ghastly looking with matted hair hanging off their bodies, long arms with long claws on their hands very sinister looking beasts they were. She told me that she has never entered the park since and would not meet me there to talk about the incident. When asked if she ever told anyone, she recalled of having told only her pastor of her church and she was told to keep the story between them. Linda assured me that I was the only other, person she had ever told.

St. Mary's Cemetery
Photo by Dewey Edwards © 2023

St. Mary's Cemetery where Dogman was digging.
Photo by Dewey Edwards © 2023

St. Mary's Cemetery where Dogman was digging.
Photo by Dewey Edwards © 2023

Lake side approach to St. Mary's Cemetery
Photo by Dewey Edwards © 2023

Death of a Hunter

Chapter 12

This particular story was one that hit home for me as it struck me hard hearing it. Because I had almost become a statistic myself in 1993. The story came to me in the year of 2000 when I was attending a 40 hour police in-serving training at a facility close to the area at a neighboring hosting Sheriff's Department. An Officer I shall call David related what had occurred in the fall of 1999. Officer David stated that he was an avid deer hunter and hunts the L.B.L. region often. That he chooses to hunt the Kentucky side believing there are more deer in that area. Officer David stated that he personally knows several of the Kentucky fish and wildlife officers that works this area. That while he was hunting in the area of Nickells Branch he had taken a break in hunting and walked out to his truck parked beside of the road. That a Park Ranger had approached him and told him they were closing this immediate area because a hunter had been just killed. Officer David was not given very much information other than for his own safety he should leave. David stated that he left the area, that he drove away and within a few miles he observed some marked vehicles and decided to approach the officers to find out more about what had happened. The officers told him that a lone hunter had been found predated upon by an unknown animal, that he had been mauled to death. No other information was given to him about the incident. Officer David stated that he did hear more about the attack approximate two weeks later, that the official report to the hunter's family was unknown animal attack, no further information was given. Officer David stated the incident never made the papers nor any news shows on local television.

Hunter massacred on TVA Right-of-way at Nickells Branch

Alert Issued to Close Road

Nickells Branch Area
Photo by Dewey Edwards © 2023

The Beasts of Mt. Pleasant Cemetery

Chapter 13

I met with witness Mike and his wife at their residence located in Cadiz, Kentucky. He had contacted me wanting to tell his encounter to someone that would investigate the incident because he had contacted local authorities whom told him he was victim to a prank or kids trying to scare them.

Mike stated that he and his wife often visits the graves of his family located at Mt. Pleasant cemetery in the L.B.L. That in the spring of 2007 they had decided to place flowers on their graves and have a small picnic. Mike said it was a very pleasant afternoon in the park. That typically they clean the headstones and place flowers next to the graves. Then they will walk a few feet away from the cemetery and spread out a blanket to talk for a while and enjoy the day together. Mike and his wife were enjoying a small afternoon picnic with sandwiches and chips and sweet tea his wife had prepared for the day. After eating their lunch, they were just talking and staring at the flowers and trees when they heard a loud howl of what he knew was not a coyote, it was much more deep and lasted longer than any normal coyote howls. This frightened his wife and even shook his nerves because it was so close to them. Mike stated they stood up and were totally shocked at what they saw next. His wife was the first to see the animal that had howled. Mike said they observed a large very tall wolf like beast standing on two legs with extremely long arms, it was almost black. The head was very large with a short snout. It was staring at them and just stood their motionless. Then all of a sudden it hunched forward moving its arms and displayed its teeth exposing large canines in a belligerent manner. As they were staring at the beast they heard noises behind them and looked toward the sound of breaking limbs in a tree. They observed another one of these beasts jump out of the tree about 50 yards from them. Mike stated he believed it had been there watching them entire time. Mike and his wife ran to their car leaving their basket and blanket, fleeing for their lives.

Mike said they never looked back and drove home when they arrived home he called the office of LBL. Police whom told him they get these kinds of pranks all the time.

Mike told me that he was fully aware of the 1982 massacre of a family of four that had taken place just down the lane in front of this cemetery and of two hunters that had been killed around the power lines past the cemetery. Mike had said that was years ago and that he simply thought they would be safe in the cemetery. He now looks at the park in a different light.

Mt. Pleasant Cemetery where Dogman was waiting in ambush.
Photo by Dewey Edwards © 2022

Marker on Trace at entrance to Mt. Pleasant Cemetery and Nickells Branch
Photo by Dewey Edwards © 2022

Road leading to 1982 "Massacre Site" near Mt. Pleasant Cemetery
Photo by Dewey Edwards © 2022

Ambush Tree at Mt. Pleasant Cemetery
Photo by Dewey Edwards © 2022

The Beasts of Redd Hollow

Chapter 14

This witness contacted me stating he lived in Bowling Green, Kentucky that he and his wife had an encounter in camp site of Redd Hollow Back Country Campground in L.B.L. The witness Jim and his wife agreed to meet with me on location within the park. This is their account.

In May of 2010 Jim and his wife met with me in Redd Hollow. Jim stated they came into the campground during the month of April 2010 they took the camp site number 2 it had trees and a view of Kentucky lake and was very pretty. Jim said they had the campground almost to themselves with only a couple of other campers. Jim and his wife had a great day at the campgrounds they took the trail that followed the park and had lots of trees and local floral spring was in the air and lots of birds and animals, very peaceful. The first night in the park was almost silent, no noise with zero car traffic. They went to sleep around 2200 hours. Jim recalled that around 0300 hours his wife awakened him stating she heard loud grunting and something big walking around the campsite. He said that they lay very still in their Airstream camper when all of a sudden a thud hit the side of it. This scared him so he yelled, 'HEY WHOS OUT THERE!' Jim did not get a reply, then they heard a loud grunting noise and their stove and pans being moved around on the concrete picnic table. He looked outside the window to see a very large creature standing outside, licking a pan it had picked up off the picnic table. Jim described what he thought was a BIGFOOT, he said it stood approximate 8 to 9 feet tall. It had short hair hanging off of it. Jim could not see it very well due to the darkness, Jim's wife was looking out the window and she screamed. The scream must have scared the BIGFOOT because it made a guttural sound and threw the pan down and simply walked off headed to the woods that surrounded the campsites. Jim said that you could actually hear the beast walk from its weight pounding the trail. That morning they packed up everything to leave. As they were preparing to exit the park Jim observed a park ranger driving in to check the sites. He approached him and told what had occurred that previous night. The park ranger told Jim he had seen a bear, that black bear frequently come down from the hills and rummage through the camps at night searching for food. Jim stated he attempted to explain to the ranger that it was not a bear, but to no avail the ranger was insistent that it was a black bear common to the area.

Jim's camp spot at Redd Hollow

Redd Hollow

The Beasts of Boswell's Landing

Chapter 15

Our next witness was a lady that lives in the area off Paris, Tn. Ms. Kathryn contacted me wanting someone to investigate or give closure to what she had encountered while camping in the L.B.L. She was happy to meet with me inside the campground at the location where she encountered what she described as the DOGMAN.

Kathryn met with me in the back- country camping area known as BOSWELL'S LANDING. She stated that her husband had died in 2018 of a heart attack. That her family had always camped at L.B.L. and she wanted to continue their tradition of family camping. Kathryn stated that in the fall of 2019 she took her two children and their family dog into the campgrounds. She wanted to try a new area to experience an area they had never been before. Kathryn parked her Coleman trailer next to the lakeshore with the woods beside of them. It was a fall day with moderate temperature and very pleasant. The campgrounds were vacant except for their small camper. She said they had spent the entire day fishing and walking the lake shore having a great day. As the sun began to set the kids and their family dog JAKE were hungry. She gathered them up and went back to camp to prepare an evening meal and melt s'mores on the fire. Kathryn cooked up some hotdogs and warmed some beans, opened a can of dogfood for JAKE and gave him some hotdogs as well. After eating their supper, they settled in by the fire to prepare some s'mores. As they were melting the marshmallows they heard some noise coming from the woods by the trail that leads to FORT HENRY. At first she believed it was probably a raccoon or opossum coming in for a bite of leftovers. Then JAKE alerted to whatever was in the woods. Kathryn stated she and her children could see two shadow figures walking behind the trees. All of a sudden JAKE began barking aggressively and took off after the figures in the woods. It was almost dark but they could see JAKE he had stopped about 30 feet from camp still barking and growling at the two figures. Kathryn stated what happened next from straight out of a horror movie that shocked them. She observed a third figure step out from behind a tree snatching up JAKE. That it looked like a large wolf that was standing on two legs, like a half man half wolf. It was holding JAKE and the dog was in great pain. The monster held up their dog and broke its neck ripping off its head. Then it just stood their showing its teeth as if it was grinning at them. Kathryn stated the children were crying and hanging onto her having seen their beloved JAKE slaughtered in front of them. The DOGMAN stared at them and took off with JAKE running in the direction of the two other shadow creatures-beasts. Kathryn grabbed the children put them into their pick-up truck and fled the campgrounds. Kathryn stated she returned the following day with a friend to retrieve their camper and personal belongings they left behind. She attempted to report the incident to authorities whom told her that what she had seen and what killed her dog was simply coyotes. That they frequent the back- country camping sites hunting for food or pets that campers bring with them. Kathryn assured me that what she and her children seen that night were bi-pedal beasts, that she believed was DOGMEN.

Entrance to Boswell's Landing Campground

Kathryn's Camp site
Photo by Dewey Edwards © 2022

Trail of the Dogman where Jake was killed.
Photo by Dewey Edwards © 2022

Boswell's Landing Shoreline
Photo by Dewey Edwards © 2022

The Author at Dogman Trail at Boswell's Landing
Photo by Dewey Edwards © 2022

The Dogman Conference of Paris, Tennessee

Chapter 16

On August 13 2022 Josh Turner and his incredible Paranormal Round Table team held a Dogman Conference in Paris only miles from the Land Between the Lakes. It was the most talented well planned conference I have ever attended. The special guests and speakers were the most experienced and revered across the earth. Let me put it like this, a building housing all of the best and most experienced folks like Josh Turner, Ken Gerhard, Barton Nunnelly, Lyle Blackburn, Ron Moorehead, Elijah Henderson, Kenny Irish and so many, many others. I was lucky enough to have been asked to appear there and speak at this conference. Joe and Jessi Doyle of HELLBENT HOLLER and the man I call the Father of paranormal encounters and investigations Barton Nunnelly had seen my interview on the movie/documentary AMERICAN WEREWOLVES by SETH BREEDLOVE and SMALL TOWN MONSTERS. They believed I could add something to the conference. Once I arrived at the conference on said day I was totally amazed at the incredible array of authors and cryptid investigators and researchers. The names of these men and women totally rocks the imagination of anyone interested in the field of Paranormal and In-humanoid encounters. As the conference was underway I was captivated by each speaker listening to each word spoken, taking in and soaking up all the wisdom and experience from these talented and well educated men and women the best of the best in their field.

But when it came time for Barton Nunnelly to speak the entire room went totally quiet you could hear a pin drop. There was not one voice nor any noise when Mr. Nunnelly took the podium. He began to tell his story of how his family had been terrorized by these In-humanoid beasts. He told of how all their farm animals had been slain, murdered by these hairy monsters from Hades itself. The crowd was silent. He then told of how his father would do anything to keep his family together at all costs, to keep his children from being taken from these hideous beasts. I tell you there was not one dry eye among the audience. Mr. Nunnelly, and his family's attack is chronicled in books and has been the subject of many television documentaries across earth. Mr. Nunnelly has been and continues to be reported by numerous investigative journalist and his stories are completely global. His books are what we refer to as the modern - day guide for all field researchers or cryptid investigators. I highly recommend anyone interested in this field to read and to buy his books. When he was done speaking the audience was in tears and filled with respect for this man and his family.

When it was my turn to speak, I thought to myself how on earth could I follow such a man, a man that I held in great reverence. I looked out into the crowd and the only thought I had was I am sharing the stage with the greatest cryptid and paranormal and in-humanoid investigator of all times, he was standing five feet from me. My only thought was that Barton Nunnelly was right beside of me I am not scared of nothing. I felt ten feet tall standing with Barton. I told my story to the public for the very first time. I looked into the crowd and observed their faces and their eyes so full of care and love. I looked out and saw my wife, for the very first time she heard my story. She had lived through my nightmares and terror but never knew why, she had attributed it to my law enforcement career, she had zero idea to what I had lived through in L.B.L. I had kept my encounter a secret from everyone including my own family. She only knew that I investigated strange encounters from others. After I spoke and told my story I also had a message, one was for the idea of public awareness and safety in our National Parks and Recreation areas. The other was to remind everyone not to ridicule or make fun of the witnesses that find the courage to come forward to tell his or her story of how they have been attacked or terrorized in fear by the sighting of these beasts or paranormal encounters. To provide a safe platform or means of sharing their stories that provides them an environment they are comfortable to speak.

Now let me come to the meat of this story and why I have included this chapter in my book. From the moment I stepped off the stage, I was humbled by my own peers,11 current serving or retired law enforcement officers greeted me before I could even take a seat. Each and every one of them presented their credentials or identification showing their serving status and thanking me for coming forward with my story. Our message was received by everyone, these Police Officers, Sheriffs and even Federal United States Deputy Marshal began to tell me they all had encounters with these types of beasts and were ready to tell the public their stories. And just as important this DOGMAN conference presented to me over 50 competent upstanding citizens / witnesses whom they had suffered encounters with these beasts what we refer to as DOGMAN or BIGFOOT creatures. And to this day at the time of writing this book witnesses continue to contact me to tell me their accounts.

I owe a huge thanks to Josh Turner and the Paranormal Roundtable team, their guests and speakers, Joe and Jessi Doyle of Hellbent Holler and most of all Barton Nunnelly.

AUTHOR'S NOTE- Over 50 witnesses have come forward to report encounters after hearing our story and continue to this present day to contact me. The majority of these witnesses are reporting encounters inside Land

Between the Lakes and surrounding areas.

Martin Groves and Barton Nunnelly on stage at the Dogman Conference

Drawing by Barton Nunnelly

Demumber's Bay

Chapter 17

Immediately after the DOGMAN conference in Paris I was contacted by three different citizens whom lived within this area. They wanted to share with me their stories. Of the three witnesses the common denominator was the fact their encounters were no other than in DEMUMBER'S BAY in L.B.L. RECREATION AREA. I should mention that there have been reports of at least 5 deaths in the very same area and another 4 deaths in the Nickells Branch creek area distal to Mt. Pleasant cemetery in the last 45 years. All of them were reported as unknown animal attacks. With reports from many researchers stating that in 1979 two campers were killed in Demumber's bay having been witnessed by a Kentucky Fish Wildlife employee from his boat. And three killed in their tents on the shore of Demumber's bay having been found by a hiker in the fall 1982. These five deaths were a stone's throw across the bay to the infamous April 7, 1982 slaying of four family members off of Nickells' branch.

Having being armed with this information and the fact that two of these reports came from encounters that took place in July of 2022 I decided to travel into L.B.L. with a field researcher and author of many paranormal and cryptid books. A man that I respect highly for his research and truthful investigations by the name of Mr. Dewey Edwards director of Cryptid and Critters Paranormal Group. We decided to investigate these reported encounters. This is what happened.

Dewey Edwards and I had been told that a husband and wife had encountered two DOGMEN on the shoreline of Demumber's bay. That they had been cruising the area in their bass boat, that the couple decided to dock their boat on the shoreline and lay out a blanket and watch the stars. It was a full moon and they had plenty of light to see into the woods behind them. The couple had been watching the stars and talking, when they both heard a loud guttural growl in the woods behind them, then crashing and breaking of tree limbs. They both stood up and began watching the woods. They saw at least two shadowy figures running between the trees, using the foliage and trees as cover. Then across the bay they heard a loud very distinct bay or howl that lasted way to long for a wolf or coyote. Then about 50 yards away one of the figures stood out from beside a tree, with only about half of its torso visible due to the foliage. It was massive, approximate 7 feet tall, completely black in color with hair not fur covering its body. At first they thought it had to be a man in a costume, it was so man-like, the bi-pedal beast then displayed its teeth, growling like a demon and showed its arms raised mid torso level, its hands or paws displaying massive claws. The couple immediately ran to their boat jumping in cranking the motor to speed off, as they were leaving they observed two beasts by the shoreline pacing back and forth by the woods. The couple left their blanket and beverages on the beach, and fled for their lives.

With the knowledge of the location of this encounter Edwards and myself began to search this area what we found was astounding to say the least.

On the beach where the couple had been we did in fact discover their discarded beverages, their blanket and a broken cell phone. The tracks left by the Beasts were massive. We took pictures of the tracks and recorded the area with photographs. In the woods above the couple we discovered many broken tree branches approximate seven to eight feet from ground to tree indicating massive creatures, each of the tracks indicating huge bi-pedal strides in the mud.

Edwards and myself continued to search the immediate area and discovered more tracks, tracks that shocked me and I have seen just about anything under the sun in Land Between the Lakes.

Before I go any further in these details, I should at least give you some idea of the fact I have been trained to track just about anything in the woods, extensive training for man or beast. The tracks we found and the story it told us was astounding.

We discovered adult and juvenile Bigfoot tracks that came from the woods line, also two huge bi-pedal canine tracks walked beside of them. They were following or trailing a large buck-deer indicated by male deer tracks. The tracks indicated they had followed the buck approximate 100 yards from the woods line, we followed the tracks to where they stopped next to the shoreline. You could see from the tracks that a great fight had taken place, where the buck had been killed, said tracks then indicated that one of the canine creatures walked heavier in the sand/mud, it was packing the slain buck. The two Bigfoot and two Dogmen had taken the buck for their meal or pleasure of the kill. Edwards recorded the area where the slaughter took place and the fact where the buck had struggled and his life was ended. We followed the tracks into the woods area for a couple of hundred yards, we stopped our tracking when it turned extremely dark. For our own safety, we decided to exit the area. We did remain in the immediate area hearing several loud powerful howls. In conclusion of this particular expedition we knew we had evidence that satisfied us both of the witnesses encounters in Demumber's bay and this was truly an active area for both BIGFOOT AND DOGMAN.

Entrance to Demumbers Bay
Photo by Dewey Edwards © 2022

Demumbers Bay
Photo by Dewey Edwards © 2022

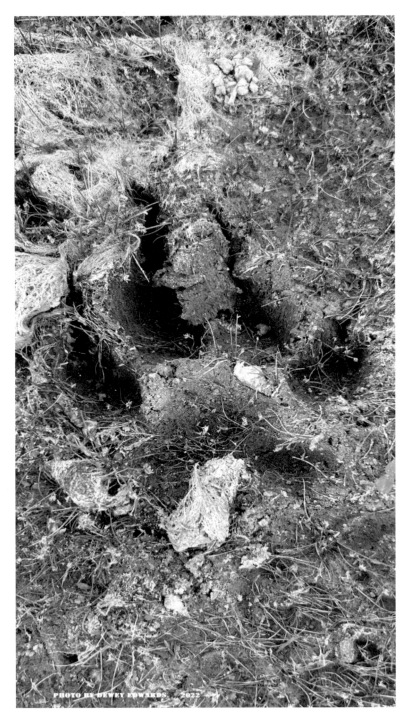

Track at Demumbers Bay
Photo by Dewey Edwards © 2022

Track at Demumbers Bay
Photo by Dewey Edwards © 2022

Track at Demumbers Bay
Photo by Dewey Edwards © 2022

Track at Demumbers Bay
Photo by Dewey Edwards © 2022

Track at Demumbers Bay
Photo by Dewey Edwards © 2022

Bigfoot Track

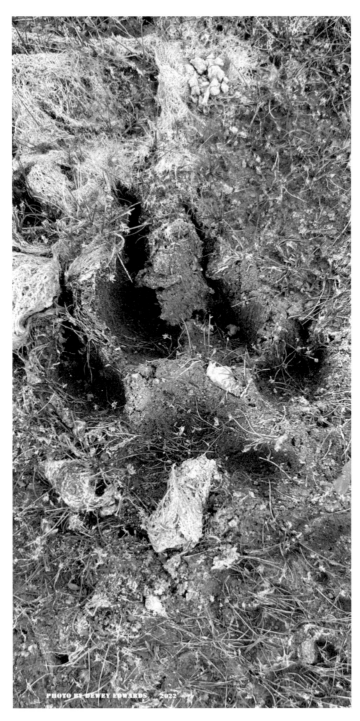

Track at Demumbers Bay
Photo by Dewey Edwards © 2022

Demumbers Bay
Photo by Dewey Edwards © 2022

Expedition 58

Chapter 18

I have personally conducted many expeditions and keep a diary of such. Since 1993 it has never been my goal to have any further encounter or contact with any paranormal, cryptid or in-humanoid creatures. Instead it has been my goal to talk with or interview any witness with the utmost reverence and assurance to protect their identity. This ensures their freedom from the ridicule and or attack from those whom either don't believe them or that wish to protect the millions of dollars of tourist revenue in this area. My goal was simple to provide a safe platform for any witness to help give them closure and find answers to why people are disappearing in our National Parks and Recreations Areas such as Land Between the Lakes. I am seeking evidence of whatever or whomever is responsible. That's my only goals. With that said to you, what takes place next was not of my desire. And to be honest with you I probably would have never ever reported it,,,,,, it would have simply gone into my diary or journal for many reasons as I have done in the past with strange encounters. I had already had an unbelievable encounter with something that should not exist. The other reason is simple I am not seeking fame nor notoriety nor recognition from these events. My only goal is to save lives in our parks I am simply seeking answers. The encounter that takes place next may have never been reported to the public because I had no explanation of what I observed nor photograph evidence to substantiate it. As well as it totally changed my way of thinking to what these Beasts were or where they lived or came from. The person that was with me felt it important enough to report it in his group that it was truly a significant sighting. And it was right to do so, I fully understand why he reported it but I had zero intentions of it being reported. With that said this is what happened on Expedition Number 58 into Land Between the Lakes.

In Oct of 2022 I entered the park with a man I had known for almost 40 years. A man I highly respect. Darrell Denton the director of BIGFOOT BELIEVERS AND OTHER CREATURES group is known for his truthfulness and his highly respected research for the phenomenon of Bigfoot and other creatures. We entered the park planning a three-day expedition that would be cut short due to the unexpected encounter with a creature of unknown origin.

Denton and myself entered the park, we had great weather for this expedition, moderate temperatures a slight breeze but heavy Chupacabra flesh blood suckers everywhere known as the infamous LBL seed ticks. We spent most of our day searching for tracks and all of the usual high traffic areas known for BIGFOOT AND DOGMAN presence. We had found numerous tracks in Demumber's Bay, a very impressive BIGFOOT handprint and several possible bedding areas. By later afternoon we took a late lunch break eating in an area noted for a recent sighting. After lunch we headed into an area close to my 1993 attack. We hiked in for a couple of miles in deep woods that opened up into food plots planted for wildlife in the area. We sat up a listening post for a few hours. During this period of time we overheard deep wood knocks that seem to surround our location, for our experience in the field this indicated to us our presence was known. We at some point decided to change our location having discovered many large adult BIGFOOT tracks in the mud around the food plots, also present were large canine prints, I mean way too large for our local inhabitant coyotes or wolves. It had become dark but we still had light to see by without using flashlights, a habit I detest in the field. If you can see at all, leave the flashlights in the pockets. Around 2000 hours we began to hear clicking sounds in the woods, coming from three different locations as if to surround us. We made a mutual decision to head back to our four - wheel drive truck. As we were walking we could hear distinct breaking of branches in the woods and hills in front of us coming toward our location, whatever it was it had to be very large to cause that much destruction or breakage in the woods. About a half mile from our truck we overheard more clicking sounds, some from the front, some from the rear. To be honest we were concerned by this, but we were both seasoned in the woods and accustom to this type of action when researching in this area. We finally made it to the truck and secured all of our gear inside, but remained outside to listen to the woods that surrounded us. We could hear a defined shrill whistle in front of us about one hundred and fifty yards ahead coming from the front of the roadway. We jumped into the truck to move to a different location on a lead I had about a sighting approximate 10 miles away. We started up the truck and headed toward the BUFFALO FLATTS. Denton and myself had traveled less than a couple of hundred yards we were traveling at a speed of approximate 5 to 10 mph. Both of us had the windows down and were watching for movement or anything in the fields or woods.

That's when our encounter took place. Denton first observed the very large creature in a deep ravine from the passenger's side of the truck. He spoke loudly and said 'DID YOU SEE WHAT I SEEN' I screamed yes. We had both observed a large beast or creature in a spider crawl in the deep ravine in a small fresh water spring/creek beside of the road. It was as if to pounce or spring up in an attack position. The beast was approximate 8 feet or greater, its color was a silver gray, more silver. It was almost in a translucent state with the outline of its body that seemed to glow almost as if I could see through the beast's body. It was very hard to make out its definite shape. As we passed I could see it stand up. Denton's description was its head was half the size of our windshield, I concur. It had a lion's mane down around its head, and a short rounded snout. But what was so defined was its eyes. Denton states its eyes were staring directly at him, as he was closest to it. The eyes seem to sit back two to three inches from its brow line, huge white glowing eyes like very bright flashlights. The beast stood up and crossed the road behind us. I could see it vividly in my mirror, it never touched the roadway, as if it either jumped or floated across it. From the driver's side of the truck I could see it traveling in the field at such speed no human could accomplish, it headed directly toward the huge hill / mountain tearing down trees and making noise as it traveled up the incline that humans would need rope and tackle and it disappeared from my view, the beast was almost as if it was translucent like. I could see through it at times. I don't know what I saw, but Denton observed the same thing. This all took place in a matter of seconds, as I am watching this travel up the hill Denton reported that his legs were numb, his head was dizzy, sick to his stomach and that he smelled something around the outside of our truck. Denton stated his throat was sore and his eyes began to well up and drip with tear drops. At the very same time I began to suffer my tongue swelling up, throat closing off, numbness to my body. My eyes were swelling and flooded with tears running down my face. I could smell the most intense acid smell like a car battery had exploded in my face. My heart and breathing rate was increased to a level as if I was having a heart attack. But the greatest pain was I could not get my airway open to receive oxygen, I could barely breathe. I floored the truck to exit the area, Denton wanted to remain in the area, but he realized I was having intense medical issues. We decided to leave the area and get to a safe location. After a few miles from the encounter we parked and discovered a very strong intense acid smell on and around our truck. It was bad enough I raised the hood of the truck to verify if the battery was leaking acid. A quick check of the truck's engine, the battery and radiator proved we had no issues. We walked around for a few minutes checking each other.

Once we were both convinced of our condition and I could breathe normal again. We began to speak of our encounter and made a decision to remain in the park, but change our location. we did remain in the park for many hours but due to my conditions, that my tongue had swollen and my eyes were affected we cut our expedition short and drove home. I personally had ill effects for days. Denton reported to me later he had returned to normal no lasting effects. Neither Denton or myself have no rational explanation for what had taken place. But I report this, the encounter took place less than two miles from my original 1993 encounter in L.B.L. My question to myself is simple, what have we discovered, is this their home, their base or fort area? Or was it the portal location of these beasts. My sincere question is WHAT LIVES IN THE DEVIL'S BACKBONE ?

Where the translucent beast emerged.
Photo by Dewey Edwards © 2022

The road where the translucent beast emerged.
Photo by Dewey Edwards © 2022

The hill where the translucent beast ascended and disappeared.
Photo by Dewey Edwards © 2022

Another view of the hill where the translucent beast ascended and disappeared.
Photo by Dewey Edwards © 2022

Another view of the hill where the translucent beast ascended and disappeared.
Photo by Dewey Edwards © 2022

The Confessionals

Chapter 19

After my last expedition into the area of the Devil's Backbone I took a few days off from the entire world. I had to regroup my senses, and collect my thoughts. How was I going to explain to others what we had observed in Demumber's Bay and the sinister Devil's Backbone areas. I had already started writing this book and wanted to include this new information to others. I had received an invitation from Tony Merkel to appear on his podcast show and do an interview, but due to my book had explained I was deep in research and interviewing witnesses that had contacted me in to report sightings in the L.B.L. region. Then in January of this year 2023 Tony Merkel extended his invitation and I decided to meet with him in his studio. I drove over to his studio just a few hours away from my location. Upon my arrival at his location I was greeted by one of the greatest individuals ever. Mr. Merkel was very kind with a wonderful personality, we hit it off immediately with so much common ground. We talked off camera concerning all of my findings and experiences and he discussed with me his beliefs and wisdom concerning the topics of BIGFOOT AND DOGMAN. The interview lasted for what seemed like only minutes but was actually hours. We spoke of so much information that we both shared with one another. I was able to tell of my story of 1993 without any time constraints. And I must be honest his level of knowledge and wisdom astounded me, and he asked the right questions of me that led me to understand the name of his show THE CONFESSIONALS. He knew by listening to me that there was indeed so much more that had occurred that night in my camp in 1993 that each event that occurred had special meaning. And we both opened up on camera about the topic of that strange metal sound that mimicked the noise of when a man had disappeared in the state of New York. And it got even more intense, the subject of what I had known for so long but could not speak of in the public. The subject of orbs and portals and how the two coincided. It was truly one of the best interviews and visits with another like-minded 'villagers' of the Missing 411 Hunter series. Tony fully knew there was something I had withheld, something so personal that both my hunting partner and I had kept to ourselves. With that said I promised Tony Merkel that I would relate the entire story within my book and appear back in his studio very soon. I would like to extend a huge thanks or Kudos to Tony for having giving me the reassurance it was time to tell Harry's story.

Image by Tony Merkel

Image by Tony Merkel

Image by Tony Merkel

Tony Merkel's studio

Harry's story

Chapter 20

As a law enforcement officer, I have interviewed thousands of witnesses or suspects in my career of over 32 years. It has been my long time experience to find that most witnesses will hold back information that is either sensitive or personal of nature. In some cases, a witness may consider vital information either worthless or insignificant to mention or simply too embarrassing for them to divulge. It sometimes takes an experienced officer or interviewer to ask the right question of a witness or suspect that will spark within them to divulge that information. In some cases, individuals will hold back believing that something they saw would or could never be deemed as believable. With my encounter in 1993 my hunting partner and myself knew that was the truth. For many years, we kept our silence right or wrong we kept our silence. We both knew that what we had observed nobody would ever believe us, the ridicule would end our careers and reputations forever more. Just before my friend's death he contacted me telling me to tell our story but leave his name out of it to spare his family from the ridicule after his death. He then left it up to me whether or not to share to others what he had personally seen. I kept that promise. After writing my book and sharing with the public what had taken place I went on a quest to search for answers and truth. Were there others whom had this type of encounter and so many other questions. There was just so much I had in my heart to search for, I had to know. I began to take small steps reaching out, searching listening and discovering. The entire time I felt I had to keep Harry's story or his part silent. I also had to keep my opinions to myself, I just could not come out and say what I thought. How could I tell others what insane things had occurred, bad enough we saw some kind of hairy furry beasts in the woods that wanted to eat us. And how was I to explain what Harry had told me that happened to him while hunting by himself. How could I explain that after years of searching for answers and what I had heard, what I had learned from others that led me to a certain realization to the hypothesis of the concepts of portals, other realms or dimensions and of mind speak. So, I ask everyone to keep all of this in mind. Here is what happened to my hunting partner Harry.

Martin and I decided to travel into the L.B.L. in the spring of 1993 for the purpose of turkey hunting. Martin had many contacts with wildlife officers and those whom worked within the park that provided great hunting areas. We loaded up my truck with our gear and food entering the park for a three- day hunt. On our first night in the park deep in the back woods we had picked a great location. We set up our camp and settled in for a supper and good night's sleep. We jumped into our bedrolls and went to sleep. Within a few hours I was awakened by a noise in our camp and was totally startled to find a large male raccoon standing on two legs beside of Martin touching his face with his paws. This startled me and I gently poked Martin for him to wake up, the raccoon stood on his hind legs and Martin woke up shewing the coon away from him. We talked for a minute and we both could not understand what had made the raccoon touch his face or be so domesticated or friendly. What was that raccoon actually doing to Martin? And was it actually a raccoon we were seeing?

The morning came and we both got out of our bedrolls preparing for the day's hunt. Martin felt it best he would take the high ridges following a game trail that led toward the hidden buffalo pastures toward the TRACE. I decided to hunt the open food plots/ fields in the area close to our camp. The fields would hold turkey that sailed down off of the high mountain / hills of the Devil's Backbone. I felt I would have a great chance of bagging the first Old Tom. The morning went without any contact with GOBBLERS only a few hens had lit in the field. It was late in the afternoon when I started experiencing the first strange contacts. I was sitting in the field using a camo netting to hide my silhouette with my back to the setting sun. I was facing a trail that came off the high ridges. The sun was still very bright so I was wearing sun glasses. I was staring at the woods when I observed two orange in color glowing orbs coming out of the high ridge line off the Devil's Backbone, traveling at moderate speed. I first believed it was my sun glasses that caused the two-round spots or orbs. I took off my glasses rubbing my eyes, looking up I observed these two orange spots or orbs that disappeared behind me on another high hill toward a cemetery located behind me a few hundred feet away. I did not know what I had seen nor did I give it any thought. Within a few minutes I heard a very loud, very strange noise coming from the area I had observed these two spots disappear. It was a metallic noise like a metal door scraping. I set for a few moments then kept hunting. Only a few minutes went by when I had some small rocks being thrown in my direction whizzing by my body landing in the corn field I was hunting. I just sit still not knowing what to think. Then an acorn hit the back of my head. I looked around but did not see anything nor anybody. Another few minutes went by when I heard a noise and a corncob flew by with great force. I turned around and at first did not see anything. It had to come from the woods line but it would have taken tremendous strength. I just kept still scanning the field and woods line. All of a sudden I saw a very tall large man walking from behind tree to tree wearing what I thought was either camouflage or a ghillie suit. That's when I realized that another hunter was in the area and he was trying to run me out of this field. I was not going anywhere, so I held my ground. I lost eye contact with any movement and could not see anyone. However, I did begin to hear loud shrill whistles coming from the area of this tall man then it was answered by another whistle high above the ridge where Martin would have been. I decided to walk back to camp as it was getting dark. Upon my arrival at camp I immediately started up the campfire. I thought about what had taken place and worried if Martin would have contact with this hunter. Over a course of time I heard what I thought to be someone hitting a tree or something, I felt it was probably Martin signaling he was coming back into camp. I relaxed a while and kept the fire going, I heard a lot of noises coming from the woods and field but could not see anything as it was very dark. I remembered the raccoon from the night before I guess I thought he was coming by to pay us another visit. As it grew later and later I did begin to worry about Martin but knew he was experienced and well- armed that he could take care of himself. As I was alone in camp I started to experience small rocks being hurled into camp, I knew Martin would never attempt to scare me as he was a serious- minded person whom would not do this. I kept my guard up with my 10 gauge side by side close to me, I also had my sidearm holstered to my hip. Within a few minutes I heard Martin say 'Hello in the camp', It was needless to say I was very happy and relieved to see him but worried as to whom was throwing pebbles or rocks at me. As Martin approached closer to camp heard him say 'I'm sorry that I have been gone so long'

I began to tell Martin what had happen to me of the strange encounter of having rocks and such thrown at me and a strange looking hunter in the woods and such. At the same time Martin began to tell me of strange large furry animals lurking between trees and strange noises, and of a man in the woods wearing a ghillie suit. We were both trying to make some sense of everything but we also shared the desire to eat supper and just settle in for the night. We came to the conclusion there must be overzealous hunters in the area or perhaps a moonshiner that we were too close to his still. But soon all our thoughts would change. As we stood in front of the campfire warming up our supper. We heard noises on the ridge above us, and noises to the east side of our camp. We thought the hunter or hunters were attempting to harass or scare us out of our camp. What takes place next happens so fast it was as if our camp or fort was being attacked. At first small twigs and rocks were coming from the ridge above us then a larger tree limb. Then I noticed something red like someone standing beside of a tree smoking a cigarette or cigar. I kept starring at the tree, and I noticed the red glow or light coming from the opposite side of the tree. Then another tree branch came off of the ridge above us. We had noises or contact coming from above us, beside of us and eventually I heard something in the field behind us. At some point Martin leaned over and whispered to me there is one or two men behind that tree smoking a stogie. I told him 'I saw em' Then a large rock came over the ridge above us, and struck the ground with a large thud. That's when Martin lost it. He started screaming at the ridge and toward the trees stating 'We are armed DEPUTY SHERIFFS you don't come into our camp like this at night, 'Come out !!!' Martin and I both heard a noise coming from the trail where he had been hunting he turned toward the trail, I picked up my shotgun and held it pointing up toward the ridgeline then toward the tree, that's when it happened.

A low very intense growl came from the trees where we thought a man had been standing hiding behind. A very intense growl that grew stronger and stronger. It seemed to penetrate my chest and body. A strong sense of fear and dread overwhelmed me, I began to get sick, nauseous to my stomach. I felt as if I was frozen unable to move or control my breathing, I felt as if I was having a heart attack due to this intense growl and humming within my ears. I could not move at some point I hurled up liquid from my stomach and felt my shoulders slump as if I was going to pass out, or hit the ground. I don't remember much from that point. The next thing I knew I, heard two rounds from Martin's weapon. I raised my shotgun and aimed at the noise and I saw two large wolf like beasts standing about seven to eight feet tall, both were standing beside of the huge tree. I discharged both barrels of my 10-gauge shotgun at them about 8 feet up, and I immediately heard screaming, loud intense howls like a pig or wolf or a mad dog. I don't know if I hit them but it sure made them mad, they ran toward the cane thicket beside of our camp and was tearing down the cane I could hear very loud screaming growls. I reached down and grabbed the gear at my feet and took off running toward the truck. I jumped into the truck and heard Martin jump into the truck bed. I started my truck and attempted to take off not realizing the parking break was on. Martin started screaming release the break hitting tho cab of my truck I turned on the headlights and immediately seen two very large beasts in the field where I had been hunting. I did not waste any time looking at them and floored the truck headed toward the creek crossing to flee out of the area. I had to slow down to cross the deep creek line when I observed creatures running beside of us, as I crossed the creek I floored the truck and hit one of these beasts as it attempted to get into the passenger's side of the truck bed and heard it scream. I fled out of the area as fast as I could Martin was in the truck bed hitting the cab, screaming for me to stop and let him. When I felt safe I stopped and he jumped in. I wanted to leave and get out of the L.B.L. but Martin convinced me to stay the night and sleep in an open field that gave us the advantage of seeing a long way for our safety. The morning came and we spoke of what had occurred I told Martin of what I had seen with the orbs and the very tall man, of the metal noises and such, Martin told me of everything that had happened to him including about meeting a firefighter whom warned him of something that circled his camp at night. That the firefighter was camped only a couple of miles away from us. We cleaned ourselves up and drove to the check station to tell our story. Upon arrival at the check station we found at least two large vans, News trucks at the station with several cameramen and news reporters present. Martin and I attempted to tell our story to the Park Rangers present but they would not listen, they insisted it had been one large bear that was sick and diseased with the mange. That it had been seen harassing other campers in the area. I attempted to show one of the Rangers the damage to my truck with claw marks down the side of it and he stated that is was definitely a bear. After being warned not to talk with the news media by the Ranger in charge we were finally told a hunter had been killed in the woods by an animal. Martin and I both believed it was the firefighter camped only a few miles away from us. That the same animals that attacked us had taken him.

After Martin and I returned home I got sicker, I went to my family doctor and learned I had suffered a stroke which had given me permanent damage and my hands that shook uncontrollably also the slurring of my speech. As a result of this attack I had to resign as a law enforcement officer unable to continue to serve. END OF STORY

You have just read the account as remembered or told by Harry to me. Some of you will understand why Harry did not want his story told, some will understand why I kept it to myself to honor Harry's wishes. Many of you will not understand nor believe what had been seen nor what we experienced. I am not here to convince you of anything. If anything at all I am here to report to you what took place. And most of all I am here attempting to warn the public and give you some idea of what is lurking in our Woods and Forrest, National Recreation Areas and National Parks and maybe just maybe find out why there is so many people that disappear without a trace, without any trace never to be seen again.

Field near Devil's Backbone
Photo by Dewey Edwards © 2022

Creek near Harry's Camp
Photo by Dewey Edwards © 2022

Martin at Rushing Creek near Harry's Camp
Photo by Dewey Edwards © 2022

The hill near Harry's Camp where the orbs appeared
Photo by Dewey Edwards © 2022

Rushing Creek Cemetery where orbs vanished near Harry's Camp
Photo by Dewey Edwards © 2022

Rushing Creek Cemetery where orbs vanished near Harry's Camp
Photo by Dewey Edwards © 2022

Standing corn near Harry's Camp
Photo by Dewey Edwards © 2022

Harry's Camp at Rushing Creek

Passing the torch

Chapter 21

I have been very blessed to meet Joe and Jessi Doyle. They came into our lives as fellow researchers or investigators in the field of Paranormal and Cryptid and U.A.P encounters. They had seen AMERICAN WEREWOLVES and later read my book BEASTS BETWEEN THE RIVERS and wanted to talk with me concerning my encounter in the L.B.L. Joe and Jessi have been very supportive and helped me to reach many people concerning the phenomenon that has touched so many lives. They are without all doubts the most professional investigators I have ever known. And I have studied with, worked with and been trained by the best experts and criminologist and police training facilities in America. This dynamic team uses the finest most modern techniques available, using modern technology and the best scientific equipment that is used for forensic investigations. The DOYLES' apply their skills in searching for clear evidence with an agenda of seeking only the truth. They obtain evidence for its value to prove or disprove the existence of the subject matter. And they report their true findings to the public. They have earned my respect many times over. This team known as Hellbent Holler are true boots on the ground, down and dirty in the woods in the forests of America. Wherever there are circumstances that warrants an investigation or research, to obtain an answer to perplexing encounters or phenomenon you will find them. I have studied their efforts as they investigate all types of these incidents and observed their many achievements. They have documented much evidence in various locations such as footprints, hair samples and photographs. Traveling into dangerous places to gather and obtain said evidence in areas where very few dare to tred at all times of the day or night, without sleep or rest, and all types of weather without any regard to their personal comfort. They are truly diehard investigators, the best of the best in my eyes. For many years, I have searched for such a team, for some one pure of heart that will search for real answers. For someone totally unafraid of the answers that they will find. If there is anyone that can or will ever find some answers to the perplexing troubles or questions we have in knowing what is in the woods and forest that attacks animals or man it shall be Joe and Jessi Doyle.

I am but an old man now, my legs can no longer can carry me due to an injury I suffered in the line of duty. I can no longer climb the hills and hollers that is necessary to chase and find the answers that we must have to prevent the loss of life in our woods. That is why I must pass the torch per say to this most trusted team. I have decided to pass any and all information that I have and all knowledge I have obtained in pursuit of these truths. Joe and Jessi Doyle, I wish you GOD'S SPEED AND PROTECTION always. DEO VINDICE!
'With GOD our protector'

Jessi and Joe Doyle of Hell Bent Holler

Image of Dogman as acquired by Hellbent Holler in LBL

Image of Dogman as acquired by Hellbent Holler in LBL

AUTHOR'S SYNOPSIS

The purpose of this book is simple. To address the issues of the missing persons that totally disappear without a trace or are found slain within our National Recreation Areas or National Parks. You will discover real life witnesses to the phenomenon of what they call the DOGMAN and BIGFOOT that is said to lurk in the shadows of Land Between the Lakes and prey upon unsuspecting visitors to the recreation area while enjoying their favorite activities. Over the course of thirty years I have met with and interviewed over two hundred witnesses. I have selected a few of these encounters for this book. The names of these witnesses have been changed to protect them from the ridicule or reprisal from those whom make their living off of the tourist trade in the region. Or from reprisal from the authorities that attempt to keep silent those whom witness the phenomenon to prevent mass hysteria or protect local tourism that brings millions of dollars of revenue to the region each year. In my book, I shall address this phenomenon and open your minds to the concept of the possibility of these beasts roaming the deep dark hollers and hills and of these lands that date back to when the American Indians call these lands home. Come join me as we discover why they called this peninsula the DARK AND BLOODLY GROUNDS. It is truly a TRACE OF DEATH.

SPECIAL THANKS

DEWEY EDWARDS my friend and brother researcher.

The DEWSTER IS THE MAN !

BARTON NUNNELLY my mentor and brother researcher whom has given everything in pursuit of truth and to help me personally to gain closure in the answers that I seek.

DARREL DENTON my friend and brother researcher

CRYPTID STUDIES INSTITUTE in memory of JOHNNY AND APRIL HENDERSON. And their children ELIJAH and GABRIELLE HENDERSON. We love you.

HELLBENT HOLLER huge thanks to my brother and sister researchers JOE and JESSI DOYLE !

There are truly so many more folks I need to give thanks to, you are truly in my hearts and I love you all.

Martin W. Groves

2023

Made in the USA
Columbia, SC
28 October 2024

44851979R00066